# Smiffy

## AND THE RUNAWAY BULL

Arcturus Publishing Limited
26/27 Bickels Yard
151–153 Bermondsey Street
London SE1 3HA

Published in association with
foulsham
W. Foulsham & Co. Ltd,
The Publishing House, Bennetts Close, Cippenham,
Slough, Berkshire SL1 5AP, England

ISBN 0-572-03087-8

British Library Cataloguing-in-Publication Data: a catalogue record for this
book is available from the British Library

This edition printed in 2005

Author: Chris Smith
Illustrator: Jim Hansen
Editor: Rebecca Gerlings

Printed in China

# Smiffy

## AND THE RUNAWAY BULL

Chris Smith
Illustrations Jim Hansen

ARCTURUS

Will and his friends were going on
a special day out.

"Come with us, Smiffy," said Will.
"Dad's taking us to Mulberry Farm!
There will be all sorts of
animals to see."

"I'd love to come!" Smiffy said,
grabbing his backpack.

Smiffy never went anywhere without his
magic backpack. He never knew when it
might come in handy.

"Now I'm ready to go," he said.

"Hello," said Farmer Joe.

"Enjoy yourselves at Mulberry Farm.

But remember to shut all gates behind you."

Smiffy nodded.

Will nodded.

Will's dad nodded.

*Everybody* nodded!
"OK, then let's go!" said Farmer Joe.

Mulberry Farm was packed with animals.
There were friendly, black-and-white cows.

And pigs who were plastered in mud…

Oink!

There were woolly sheep…

Baaaaa!

And tiny newborn lambs…

"There's one
animal left to see,"
said Farmer Joe.

Smiffy wondered what it could be. A fluffy chick? A grumpy goat? A galloping horse?

The farmer pointed to a huge field.
"Here he is!" he said.

Smiffy looked
left and right.
But the field
was empty.

"Oh, no!" shouted Farmer Joe, angrily.
"Someone's left the gate open. He's escaped!"

Will gasped.

Ella
squealed.

Alfie jumped.

But Smiffy stayed calm. He was puzzled.
*Who* had escaped?

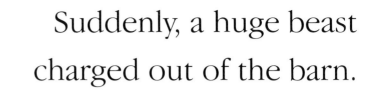

Suddenly, a huge beast
charged out of the barn.

It was a bull!

It had big eyes,
big nostrils
and a big ring
through its nose.

Everyone ran to hide…

…except Smiffy.

He stood right where he was
and opened his backpack.

A puff of magical sparkles appeared from inside it, followed by…

...an *enormous* red flag.

The bull stopped running.

He stared at Smiffy who held the flag
up high above his head.

Then, Smiffy began to do the strangest dance.

He swooshed
the flag around
his head.

He jumped up,
down, up, down.

Then he hopped
and skipped
towards the field.

The bull stared. He snorted and he stamped his feet.

Then he
plodded slowly
after Smiffy…

…nearer and nearer to the field.

Farmer Joe clanged the gate shut behind the big bull.

Clang!

And Smiffy jumped back over the gate.

"Well done, Smiffy!" shouted everyone.

Smiffy grinned. It was time for tea.
Adventures always made him hungry.